Words to Know Before You Read

chair
champion
cheese
cheesy
cherry
chewy
chicken
children
chili
chips
chowder

www.rourkeeducationalmedia.com

Edited by Precious McKenzie
Illustrated by Ed Myer
Art Direction, Cover and Page Layout by Tara Raymo

Library of Congress PCN Data

The Chili Challenge / Meg Greve
ISBN 978-1-62169-268-3 (hard cover) (alk. paper)
ISBN 978-1-62169-226-3 (soft cover)
Library of Congress Control Number: 2012952773

Rourke Educational Media
Printed in the United States of America,
North Mankato, Minnesota

Rourke
Educational Media

rourkeeducationalmedia.com

customerservice@rourkeeducationalmedia.com • PO Box 643328 Vero Beach, Florida 32964

Chili Challenge

Counselor
Gus

Counselor
Mindy

Fitz

Dex

Lizzie

Ana

Written By Meg Greve
Illustrated By Ed Myer

"I'm hungry," whines Fitz.

"I wish I had some cheese puffs," says Lizzie.

"I want some chewy, cheesy chicken bites," says Dex.

"Let's go to the Kids' Food Festival," says Counselor Gus.

"Climb in!" says Counselor Mindy.

"Buckle up for a bouncy ride!" calls Counselor Gus.

CAMP ADVENTURE

Kids Food Festival

"I want a piece of cherry cheesecake," says Ana.

Lizzie chimes in, "Yummy, crunchy chips for me."

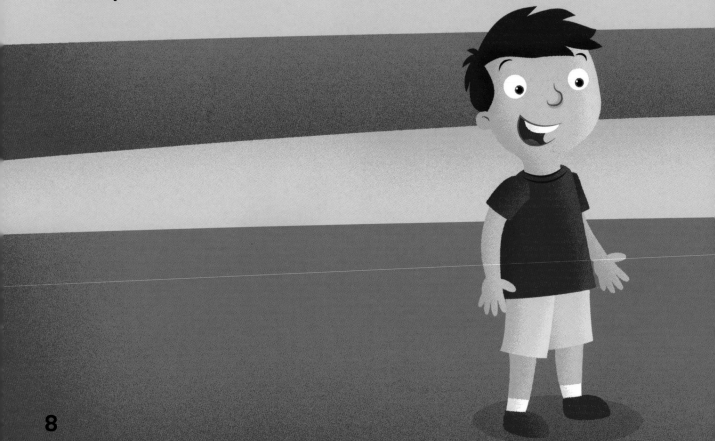

CHERRY
CHEESECAKE

CRUNCHY
CHIPS

"Look at the pots of prize winning chili," says Counselor Mindy.

"I want a chance to try all the chili," says Fitz.

All the children slurp and chew and munch and crunch.

There is cheese dripping on the chair and mustard in Dex's hair.

But where is Fitz?

He has entered the Chili Eating Challenge!

He takes a scoop from the first bowl.

He chomps and chews.

"Too cheesy," he says.

He chomps and chews some more.

"Tastes like chowder," says Fitz.
Then he tries another bowl of chili.

"HOT! HOT! HOT!" shouts Fitz.

The judge gives him a trophy.
Fitz is the new chili eating champion!

After Reading Word Study

Picture Glossary

Directions: Look at each picture and read the definition. Write a list of all of the words you know that start with the same sound as *chili*. Remember to look in the book for more words.

chair (CHAIR): A chair is something you can sit down on and rest.

champion (CHAM-pee-uhn): A champion is the winner of a contest.

cheese (CHEEZ): Cheese is a dairy food made from milk.

cherry (ch-AIR-ee): A cherry is a small fruit with a pit in it. Cherries grow from trees.

chicken (CHIK-uhn): A chicken is a bird that is used for meat and eggs. The meat that comes from the bird is called chicken.

children (CHIL-druhn): Children are a group of young people.

About the Author

Meg Greve lives in Chicago with her husband and her two kids named Madison and William. They love to eat chili – hot, cheesy, and spicy! Yum!

Ask The Author!
www.rem4students.com

About the Illustrator

Ed Myer is a Manchester-born illustrator now living in London. After growing up in an artistic household, Ed studied ceramics at university but always continued drawing pictures. As well as illustration, Ed likes traveling, playing computer games, and walking little Ted (his Jack Russell).